AuthorHouse™
1663 Liberty Drive
Bloomington, IN 47403
www.authorhouse.com
Phone: 1 (800) 839-8640

Published by AuthorHouse 04/08/2019

ISBN: 978-1-7283-0565-3 (sc)
978-1-7283-0567-7 (hc)
978-1-7283-0566-0 (e)

Library of Congress Control Number: 2019903539

Print information available on the last page.

authorHOUSE®

Detective Byrd
in the Case of the Missing Brain

Written and Illustrated by
Monica Lea Maxfield

You QUIT what?

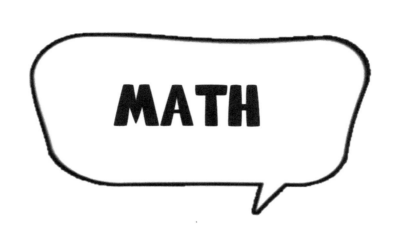

I'M TIRED!
IT'S TOO HARD!
I'M CONFUSED!

My Poor
Brain
needs
a doctor!

Ouchy!

Woe is me!

Maybe your brain needs a vacation...

...or maybe your brain took
a vacation and forgot to
tell you...

Where are we going?

We are going to go find your brain

Where do you think you left it last?

Well, I started to work
on my math problems
this morning....

So we know it happened today...

Let's take a look at
those math problems.
Maybe they will give us a clue.

Now, you say your brain
started to hurt when
you were trying to do math..

Then what?

That's when I screamed

"I QUIT!"

I see...so, your brain didn't take a vacation, it just walked off the job.

Maybe your
brain is
tired and needs
a little nap...

Sometimes, all you have to do is kiss your brain and let your brain know that you love your brain.

Sometimes all your brain needs
is a little encouragement.

Sometimes, all your brain needs a little

"**PEP** talk".

Okay brain, you know you can do this...

$$2 + 3 = 5$$
$$7 + 3 = 10..$$

Let's hear it for your brain!
Three cheers! You can do it!
Yes you can! If you can't do it!
No one can!! RAH! RAH! RAH!
Way to go Brain!!

I DID IT!
I DID IT!

EASY
PEEZY
LEMON
SQUEEZY!

I knew you could do it!
Way to go Hermmy!

Thanks Julie.
Your'e a good friend.

Don't thank me.
Thank your brain.

The End

Comprehension Questions:

What does Julie do to encourage Hermmy?

A) Tell him "it's no big deal.

B) Cheer him on.

C) Give him a snack.

Comprehension Questions:

Why is Hermmy crying?

A) His brain hurts.

B) Someone took his cookie.

C) Someone hurt his feelings.

Comprehension Questions:

What does Hermmy need help with?

A) Reading

B) Writing

C) Math

On my own Question:

How could you help your friend if they got stuck on a math problem?

A) Encourage them.

B) Do the work for them.

C) Tell them to try to solve the problems themselves.

On my own Question:

If you got stuck on a math problem, who would you ask?

A) Shoulder partner.

B) My teacher.

C) Nobody, I got this!

On my own Question:

How many tricky words could you read?

A) 1

B) 4

C) All of them!

Detective Byrd: Case # 101

CPSIA information can be obtained
at www.ICGtesting.com
Printed in the USA
BVHW020327300519
549348BV00053B/2681/P

9 781728 305653